nighttime ninja

By Barbara DaCosta ✷ Art by Ed Young

SCHOLASTIC INC.

The clock struck midnight....

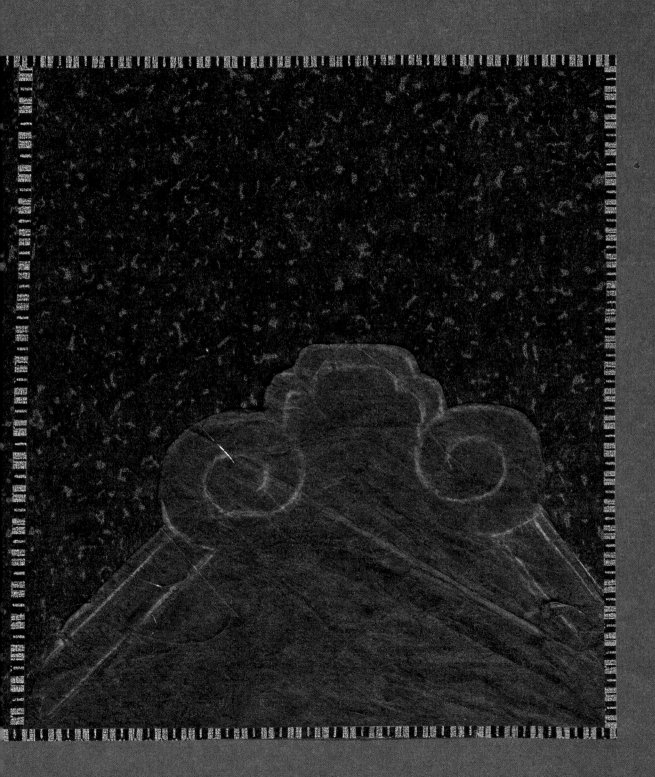

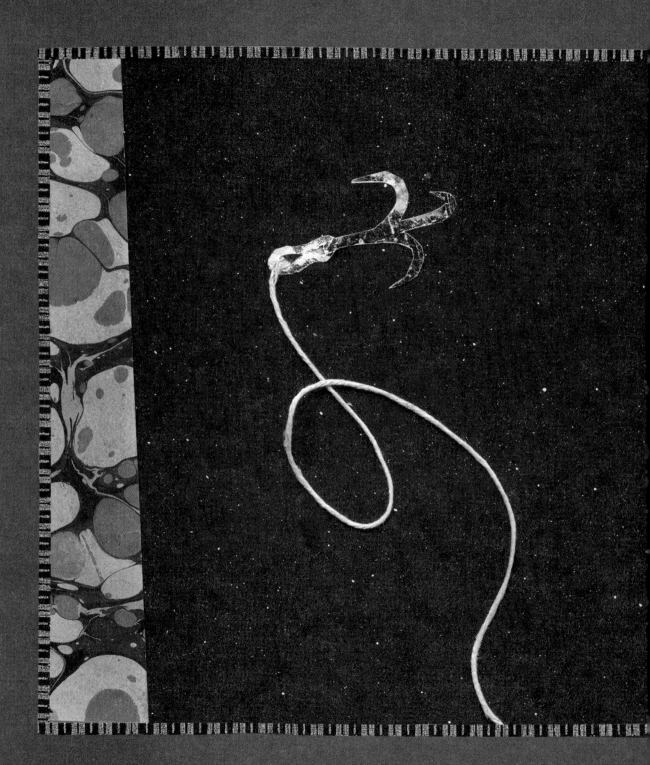

Hand over hand,

the ninja climbed and clambered.

Step by step,

he balanced and leapt.

The house
was silent.
Everyone
was asleep.

He crept down the
twisting moonlit hallway,

and knelt in the
dark shadows,
listening.

Wait—look!

He took out his tools

and went to work.

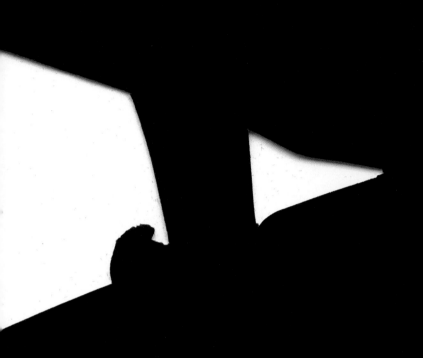

Suddenly, the lights flashed on!

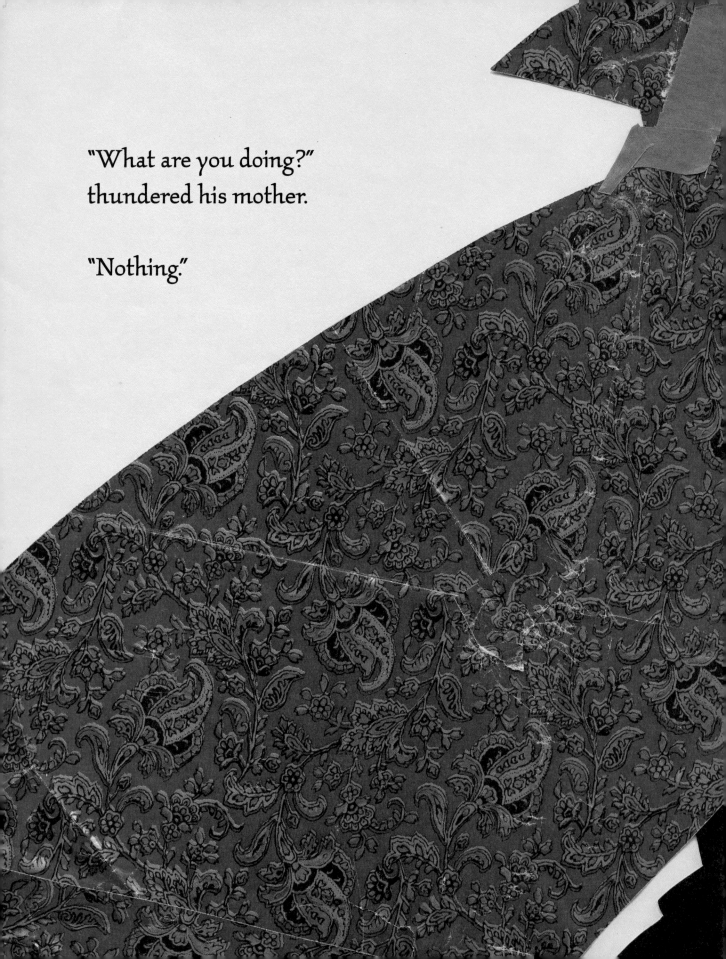

"What are you doing?"
thundered his mother.

"Nothing."

"Hand it over, mister."

"But I'm not done with my mission yet."

"Well, how about a getting-back-into-bed mission?"

"Sweet dreams,
Nighttime Ninja."

The illustrations for this book were done in cut paper, textured cloth, string, and colored pencil.
The text was set in Kallos, and the display type was hand-cut.

In memory of my mother:
the power of the mind, the warmth of the heart
—B.D.

To mystery, which holds our imagination hostage
in delight of its suspense and anticipation
—E.Y.

As a child, **Barbara DaCosta** was a precocious nighttime ninja, constantly climbing out of her crib in search of cookies and other interesting things. She has since cut back on the climbing and the cookies but still enjoys finding the interesting things in life to write about. *Nighttime Ninja* is her first children's picture book. She makes her home in Minneapolis, Minnesota.

Ed Young is the illustrator of more than eighty books for children, including the Caldecott Medal–winning *Lon Po Po* and the *New York Times* bestseller *Wabi Sabi* by Mark Reibstein. Ed also wrote and illustrated *The House Baba Built*, which recounts his childhood in Shanghai. Born in China, he moved to the United States as a young man and pursued his love of art. *Nighttime Ninja* is the type of picture book Ed would have loved as a young boy. He currently lives in New York.